DATE DUE			

W9-CFH-046

MY FIRST
I Can Read Book®

Mine's the Best

BY CROSBY BONSALL

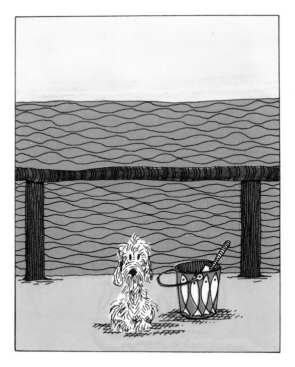

HarperCollinsPublishers

HarperCollins®, 📖®, and I Can Read Book®
are trademarks of HarperCollins Publishers Inc.

Mine's the Best
Copyright © 1973 by Crosby Bonsall
Copyright © 1996 by the Estate of Crosby Bonsall
Manufactured in China. All rights reserved.

Library of Congress Cataloging-in-Publication Data
Bonsall, Crosby Newell, 1921–1995
    Mine's the best / by Crosby Bonsall.
        p.   cm. — (My first I can read book)
    "Newly illustrated edition."
    Summary: Two little boys meet at the beach, each sure that his balloon is
better.
    ISBN 0-06-027090-X. — ISBN 0-06-027091-8 (lib. bdg.)
    ISBN 0-06-444213-6 (pbk.)
    [1. Friendship—Fiction.]   I. Title.   II. Series.
PZ7.B64265Mi   1996   95-12405
[E]—dc20   CIP
                                                                     AC

❖
Newly Illustrated Edition

Mine's the Best

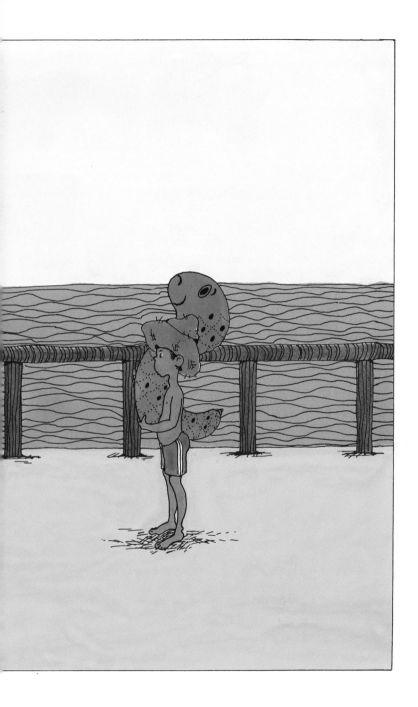

"Mine is the best."

"It is not.

Mine is."

"Mine has more spots."

"It does not.

Mine has."

"Well, mine is bigger."

"It is not.

Mine is."

"Mine can stand up."

"Mine can too."

"Mine can sit
on my head."

16

"Mine can sit

on MY head."

17

"I can ride mine."

"I can ride mine better."

"Yours is sick."

"So is yours."

"Yours is very sick."

"So is yours."

"Yours is dead."

"Yours is dead too."

"It's all your fault."

"No, it's all YOUR fault."

"Let go of my pants."

"Let go of my hat."

"She thinks

she's smart!"

"I hate her."

"Ours was the best."